Out There?

MYSTERIOUS SIGNS

John Townsend

Chicago, Illinois

© 2004 Raintree
Published by Raintree,
A division of Reed Elsevier, Inc.
Chicago, IL

For information, address the publisher:
Raintree, 100 N. LaSalle, Suite 1200, Chicago, IL 60602
Printed and bound in China
08 07 06
10 9 8 7 6 5 4 3 2

Library of Congress Cataloging-in-Publication Data:
Townsend, John, 1955-
  Mysterious signs / John Townsend.
        p. cm. -- (Out there?)
Includes bibliographical references and index.
Contents: Signs and wonders -- Carved on the Earth -- Secrets of the stones -- Power of the pyramids -- Mystery of the mounds -- Dents and dimples -- What on Earth will we look like?
  ISBN 1-4109-0566-7 (Lib. binding), 1-4109-0967-0 (Pbk.)
  1. Curiosities and wonders--Juvenile literature. [1. Curiosities and wonders.] I. Title. II. Series: Townsend, John, 1955- Out there?
  AG243.T67 2004
  001.94--dc21

                              2003010545

Acknowledgments
The publishers would like to thank the following for permission to reproduce photographs: pp. 6 (bottom), 8 (bottom), p. 10 (bottom), 20 (left), 24–25 Fortean Picture Library; p. 10 (top) F. C. Taylor/Fortean Picture Library; pp. 6 (top), 21, 30–31, 36, Corbis; p. 8 (top) Christopher Cormack/Corbis; p. 9 Terence Meaden/Fortean Picture Library; p. 11 Weetabix Ltd.; p. 12–13 Steve Alexander/Rex Features; p. 12 British Film Institute; p. 13 Buena Vista International; pp. 14–15 Chris Beall/Lonely Planet; pp. 15, 22, 30–31, 48–49, 50 Photodisc; pp. 17 (left), 28, 40 Klaus Aarsleff/Fortean Picture Library; p. 16 Lonely Planet; pp. 18–19, 39 Yann Arthus-Bertrand/Corbis; p. 18 Angelo Hornak/Corbis; p. 19 Alamy Images/Corbis; p. 20 (right) Roman Soumar/Corbis; p. 22–23 Niall Benvie/Corbis; p. 23 Richard Nowitz/Corbis; p. 24 Hubert Stadler/Corbis; p. 25 Rob Pilgrim; p. 26 James Amos/Corbis; pp. 26–27 Kevin Schaefer/Corbis; p. 27 Ric Ergenbright/Corbis; pp. 28–29 Fortean Picture Library/Dr. Elmar Gruber; p. 29 Bill Ross/Corbis; pp. 30, 31 Peter Evans; p. 34 RSPCA Photo Library; pp. 34–35 Staffan Widstrand/Corbis; pp. 36–37 Danny Lehman/Corbis; pp. 38 (right), 40–41 Richard A. Cooke; p. 41 Paul Souders/Corbis; p. 42 David Muensch/Corbis; pp. 42–43 Getty Images Taxi; p. 43 John Miles; p. 44 Ronald Grant Archive; pp. 44–45 Charles O'Rear/Corbis; pp. 45, 46 (top), 47, 49 Science Photo Library; p. 46 (bottom) Dazso Sternoczky/SUFOI/Fortean Picture Library; p. 48 (left) U.S. Geological Survey/Science Photo Library.

Cover Photograph of Stonehenge used with permission of Corbis.

CONTENTS

Any words appearing in the text in bold, **like this,** are explained in the glossary. You can also look for them in the "Weird Words" box at the bottom of each page.

WHAT ON EARTH DO WE LOOK LIKE?

Our planet is full of secrets. These secrets have puzzled **humankind** for years, yet little has ever been explained. Why do some places hold such strange powers? Can puzzles from the past help unravel some of Earth's mysteries?

Eyes looking down from space may see far more than we ever will.

THE VIEW FROM ABOVE

People often see weird and mysterious things. Seeing these things from the ground is strange enough. But when we look down on Earth from the sky, we can see even more amazing sights.

ALIEN LIFE?

Perhaps the strange marks we can see on Earth are signs that aliens once visited our planet. They could be signs that others have been here before us. If so, who? Why did they leave these marks, and what do they mean?

HIDDEN POWERS

Science cannot explain all of Earth's mysteries. Even though we now understand some of the signs we once thought were alien, there are still unanswered questions. What powers does our planet hold? What forces are at work?

There may be much more to these mysteries than meets the eye.

FIND OUT LATER...

What made these signs in the fields?

Is this a runway for alien spacecraft?

What are the secret signs of the pyramids?

pyramid   large stone monument with sloping sides and a point

SIGNS AND WONDERS

STRANGE SHAPES

Crop circles come in all shapes and sizes: keys or claws, weird insects, stars in space . . .

Crop circles are flattened areas in cornfields. They often appear overnight in the shape of circles or other designs. But what makes them? Are they:

- The result of the weather?
- Jokes made by people?
- The marks of aliens? Perhaps there are other secrets behind these circles. They may be more mysterious than we think.

Many crop markings are in the shape of keys. **‹‹**

Could humans really create designs like this at night, without anyone noticing?

WEIRD WORDS   fraction   small part of the total
sacred   special in a religious way

WEIRD PATTERNS

Strange shapes in crops have puzzled us for hundreds of years. They have only been studied in detail in the last 30 years. Since we have been able to take photos from the sky, we have begun to see them better and wonder more about them.

WHAT ON EARTH ARE THEY?

Some circles show amazing designs. Are they **sacred symbols**? Are they trying to tell us something? Are there strange forces at work? There are plenty of ideas out there about what the patterns really are.

Thousands of crop circles have appeared in Wiltshire, England, in the last 50 years.

WHERE ON EARTH ARE THEY?

You can often see these strange designs in cornfields. But the patterns are not only found in fields of crops. You can also see them in grass, sand, soil, snow, and ice. Sometimes they appear in leaves on trees.

In fact, they may be all around us, but we cannot always see them. We may see only a **fraction** of these strange "fingerprints."

Fast Fact
Crop circles have appeared in Australia, Britain Canada, Israel, Japan, South Africa, the U.S., and about 40 other countries.

HOT SPOTS

Crop circles seem to "crop up" all over the world. But they appear in some areas more often than others. Wiltshire, England, is one of the hottest spots for crop circles every year.

symbol   sign with a meaning

- The earliest crop circle on record appeared in Assen, Holland, in 1590.

- The largest crop circle filled a whole field—over 360 yards (330 meters) across.

In some crop circles, microphones have stopped working correctly.

DESIGN

The amazing thing about these circles is their design. They are all different and some are very **complex.** It is hard to believe they just happen by chance. Someone must have planned each part. Every line seems to fit and every little shape plays its part in the whole design. The full effect is hard to see from the ground.

WHIRLWINDS

Some scientists think the weather may play a part in making the circles. Perhaps the flow of air over hills may make mini-whirlwinds. These winds could be charged with electricity. This could explain why some people have seen lights or heard humming around crop circles.

Crop circles have to be seen from above.

magnetic   related to the forces of the North and South Poles

REED CIRCLES

Although strange circles may have appeared long ago, they have only been **examined** in recent years. In Australia, people only began to notice strange shapes in swamps in the 1960s. These circles of **reeds** appeared in some swamps. Then people saw patterns in the fields nearby.

FOREST CIRCLES

Hundreds of forest circles have appeared in northern Canada. They can only be seen from the air, and some are over 1.25 miles (2 kilometers) across. One idea is that electrical energy inside Earth may make the trees grow in this way. But no one knows for sure what is really behind the patterns.

A SURGE OF POWER?

We have always known that Earth has some amazing forces:

- electrical energy;
- **magnetic** fields;
- **radiation**.

Perhaps they may explain some crop patterns. We are still finding out how these forces affect us and our planet.

Could mini-whirlwinds make crop circles?

radiation   invisible waves of energy that can be harmful in high doses
reed   plant with tall stalks that grow in water

MARKS BY HUMAN HANDS

Strange air currents cannot explain how all crop circles form. Many people think that they are human-made. Crop circles often appear in the early morning in **remote** places. We now know that many crop circles are made by people. Some are done as a **hoax.** Others are done as a form of crop art.

This pattern seems too **complex** to be a hoax.

MYSTERY

Can all crop circles be made by humans overnight? Experts do not know how this strange design was made on Milk Hill in Wiltshire, England in 2001. It had 409 circles and was nearly 984 feet (300 meters) across. That would take many people all day to make.

Humans can make crop circles, but it takes a long time.

Experts have studied bent stalks and soil inside crop circles. Sometimes they find higher **magnetic** readings inside the circles than outside. It is still hard to prove if humans have made the pattern or if it is made by something else.

alien being from out of this world
hoax   joke, trick, or something that is not real

HOAX

So how do you make a crop circle? The tools are simple: a wooden stake, a rope, some boards, and a few people.

In 1978 Doug Bower and his friends began the craze of making crop circles. Doug had lived in Australia when circles first appeared in Queensland. Stories spread about **alien** spacecraft landing in the area. Doug had not made any crop circles before, but he decided to make some in England. It would be fun to see if people thought a flying saucer had landed. His joke worked. People went wild. For over twelve years, Doug's group of circle-makers fooled many people. There may be many more jokers out there today.

CEREAL SIGNS

In July 2002 people made a huge crop design for Weetabix, a British cereal. It took three men several days to "map out" the design and a total of sixteen hours to finish it. "It must be the most difficult we have ever been asked to make," they said.

The Weetabix crop design was in the shape of an electrical outlet. **《《**

MEL GIBSON

M. NIGHT SHYAMALAN'S

signs

This 2002 Disney movie raised a lot of interest in crop circles and their link with aliens.

SIGNS

Signs is a thriller set in Bucks County, Pennsylvania. Mel Gibson stars as a farmer who discovers crop circles on his farm. He tries to find the truth behind the mysterious circles. There are noises in the night and he sees figures in the moonlight. But that is just the beginning. . . .

ARE WE ALONE?

Crop circles often appear in **UFO** hot spots. People have even reported seeing UFOs hovering over crop circles. But there is still no real proof of this. If **aliens** make crop circles, the question is: Why are they doing it? There are three ideas :

- The circles are landing sites for alien spacecraft. "Flying saucers" flatten the crops where they land.
- The patterns are messages from aliens. They might be a way of saying "hello" or a warning in code.
- The markings are maps and signs that are made and used by aliens. They may help aliens to find their way or to signal to other aliens.

This bird formation appeared in a field in Wiltshire, England.

   UFO   unidentified flying object

STRANGE SIGNS IN UTAH

In 1996 Seth Alder was about to harvest his wheat in Utah when his tractor broke down. It was then he saw a strange shape cut into his field. There was no sign of anyone having walked in the field. No wheat was broken or stepped on. Then strange lights appeared above the circle at night. It was thought this was the first recorded crop-circle light in the United States.

Many thought it was the work of UFOs, which are said to make tractors, cameras, or cell phones stop working. Farm animals have been noisy and nervous on nights when crop circles form nearby.

A PLACE TO STAY

Would you believe that crop circles can make a good love story? The 2002 film *A Place to Stay* was made in Wiltshire, England. The two main characters in the film meet because they both like finding new crop circles.

The subject of "crop signs" is now good business for movies.

A MARCUS THOMPSON

COLM Ó MAONLAÍ

AMANDA RAY KING
MIRANDA LLEWELLYN JENKINS

a PLACE to STAY

WINNER
GAIA FILM AWARD 2003
for environmental awareness - drama

HOLLYWOOD DAZE MOTION PICTURES presents a MARCUS THOMPSON FILM starring COLM Ó MAONLAÍ AMANDA RAY KING JOHNNY DALLAS MIRANDA LLEWELLYN JENKINS director of photography MIRKO BEUTLER art director PETER KING chief consultant COLIN ANDREWS associate producers DERMOT RICE & DOUG BROWN produced written and directed by MARCUS THOMPSON cameras & lenses PANAVISION color by deluxe

CARVED ON THE EARTH

PERU'S SCRATCHPAD

The Nazca Plain is very dry and flat. With no sand to cover the plain and little rain or wind, lines drawn in the ground do not rub away. It is like a huge writing pad for artists who wanted to leave their mark forever.

There are strange lines in the desert of Peru in South America. They are scratched in the ground at Nazca. But it was not until people looked down from aircraft that we knew about these markings. About 300 designs can only be seen fully from the air. They make huge pictures of animals, birds, fish, and insects. Some of the animal drawings are more than two soccer fields long. The big mystery is: Why are they there? The markings may be 1,500 years old. No one really knows how or why they were made.

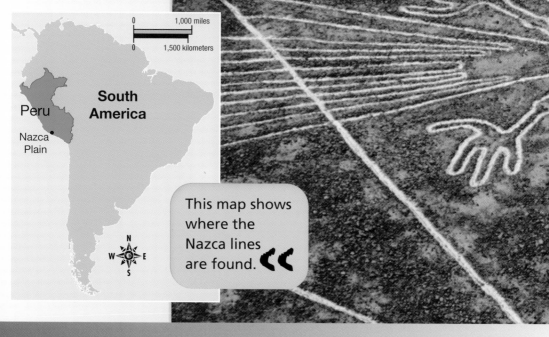

0 1,000 miles

0 1,500 kilometers

South America

Peru

Nazca Plain

N W E S

This map shows where the Nazca lines are found. **‹‹**

image   drawing or shape made to represent an object

THE ARTISTS

Nazca Indians may have made the Nazca lines. They lived in the area between 300 B.C.E. and 800 C.E. Their pottery has been found around the lines. We know very little about these people and why they would want to draw such lines and shapes. In total there are about 800 miles (1,300 kilometers) of straight lines. Some are very narrow and others are hundreds of miles wide. There are triangles, zigzags, and spirals. But most amazing are the drawings of a great spider, a monkey, and a whale. The **image** of the humming bird must be the biggest picture there is of the smallest bird in the world.

The Nazca spider is 148 feet (45 meters) wide!

THE PUZZLE

Since the Nazca lines were found 80 years ago, many scientists have tried to study their meaning. One of them was Maria Reiche, who spent over 50 years studying the drawings. She said, "We will never know all the answers. That is what a good mystery is all about."

Whoever created the Nazca lines drew many of the animals of the area. This is a hummingbird. **‹‹**

WHO IS IT?

In 1982 another drawing was found at Nazca. It is a huge man, 105 feet (32 meters) long. It is often called "the Astronaut." Is it an alien? Maybe it is an image of a god. Whatever it is, was it drawn as a sign to something "up there"?

SIGNS TO SPACECRAFT?

The signs in the Nazca desert raise two big questions. Since the lines need to be seen from the sky, did the Nazca Indians know how to fly? Or did they draw their huge pictures for **UFOs**? Another mystery has never been solved. Did **ancient** people know how to make and fly hot-air balloons? Pottery found in Peru shows **images** of what may have been balloons or kites. There are also what seem to be burn marks in the desert. These blackened rocks at the end of the lines may have been the **launch sites** for hot-air balloons. Or were they the landing sites of UFOs? We may never know.

This Nazca marking is called "the Astronaut." It is probably a drawing of a human or a god.

Key
1 Killer whale
2 Wing
3 Baby condor
4 Bird
5 Animal
6 Spiral
7 Lizard
8 Tree
9 Hands
10 Spiral
11 Spider
12 Flower
13 Dog
14 Astronaut
15 Triangle
16 Whale
17 Trapezoids
18 Star
19 Pelican
20 Bird
21 Trapezoid
22 Hummingbird
23 Trapezoid
24 Monkey

WEIRD WORDS   astronomy   study of space and the night sky
baffle   to confuse and mystify

THE GREAT RUNWAY

Some scientists think the lines across the desert are related to the Moon and stars. Perhaps the Nazca Indians drew them to study **astronomy.** But one of the shapes has **baffled** experts for years. It is an arrowlike triangle more than half a mile long. Some people think it could have been a runway for **alien** spaceships.

Some writers describe the markings as being signs to other aliens. Perhaps "the runway" was drawn to help others find their way. The shape of the lines is just right for a landing strip.

OTHER SIGNS

The Nazca lines are not the only large drawings scratched on the ground. Others have appeared from California to Chile. But the drawings at Nazca are special. They are very large, with about 300 of them packed into an area of 310 sq. miles (500 sq. kilometers).

Are the Nazca lines proof that visitors from space came to Earth many years ago?

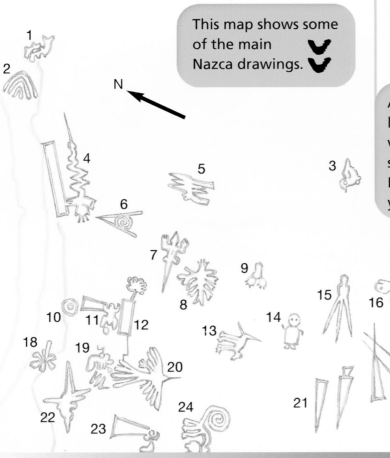

HORSES IN THE HILLS

Is there a link between crop circles and hill carvings? Wiltshire, England, has many of both. Perhaps ancient people felt a special energy from Earth here. They may have met in large numbers at their **sacred** white horses to feel Earth's mystery.

WHITE HORSES

Long ago, people carved shapes into hills. They chose a hill with chalky ground, cut away the grass and turf, and the white chalk underneath showed through. They could make pictures of animals on the hillsides, and the most common shape was a large, white horse. There are still many of these horses on English hills, but they are also found all around the world.

SIGNS ON THE HILLS

But why did people make these pictures? Were they trying to signal to someone? Some **ancient tribes** were known to **worship** a horse god. Perhaps these signs on the hills were simply to please the gods.

The Uffington Horse is one of the oldest carvings in the world. >>

fertility   ability to give birth
tribe   group with similar beliefs who live together

SHROUDED IN MYSTERY

The White Horse of Uffington near Oxford, England, is one of the oldest shapes carved into hills. Scientists think it could be 3,000 years old. Its design is different from all others. It is 360 feet (110 meters) long. This is much larger than other hill markings. It can be seen clearly from 20 miles (32 kilometers) away or from the sky.

There is still much mystery about this white horse. No one knows why it was made all those years ago. Did a local tribe cut it out of the soil as a way to signal to others? Some chalk figures may have been used for magic or as signs to bring **fertility.**

THE WHITE HORSE OF CHIHUAHUA

There is not much mystery about this modern horse on a Mexican mountain. It is a huge copy of the Uffington horse that faces to the left instead of to the right. It is over 0.3 miles (0.75 kilometers) long. It was painted in **whitewash** over three years by Hector Acosta.

The Osmington white horse in England is the only one to have a rider. It was made in 1808.

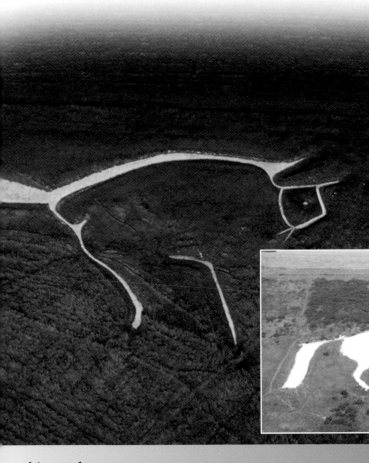

GIANTS IN THE DUST

The largest human figure at Blythe is 187 feet (57 meters) from head to toe. It has some sort of animal nearby. But what is it telling us? The drawings are now fenced in to stop further damage from tires or feet.

SECRETS OF THE PAST

In 1931 a pilot flying along the Colorado River saw giant drawings on the desert floor near Blythe, California. The **images** were faint, but one of the figures was about 200 feet (60 meters) long. Since then, over 600 drawings have been found across the southwestern United States and Mexico.

SIGNS ON THE PLAINS

The drawings are called the Blythe **Intaglio** (pronounced *in-tal-yoe*). *Intaglio* means "a carving." No one knows who made these carvings in the ground. They may be 200 or 10,000 years old, and they show patterns, people, and animals. Although many have survived wind and rain, others have been destroyed. Motorcycles, all-terrain vehicles, and tanks churning up the ground have not helped.

We cannot explain why ancient peoples carved giant human figures onto the earth.

This strange candlestick is carved onto a hill in Peru.

ancestors   people from the past from whom someone has descended

RIDDLES

There are Native Americans living along the Colorado River. Perhaps their **ancestors** made these signs on the plains. Mohave Indians could have made them. Yet present day Mohave do not think this is so.

Perhaps the drawings are messages to **ancient** people's gods or ancestors. Or maybe the pictures tell stories—like a giant comic book. These Earth drawings remain a mystery. But just as one pilot found the Blythe Intaglio over 70 years ago, many more may still be waiting to be spotted from the air. And we will never know how many have already been dug up and lost forever.

FISHERMAN

In the **foothills** of the Plomosa Mountains in Arizona is a drawing called "the Bouse Fisherman." He has a spear and two fish below him and a sun and a snake above him. He is very hard to find and a long way from any water.

> Native Americans may have drawn the most important parts of everyday life, such as catching food. **‹‹**

foothills   low hills around the base of a mountain
intaglio   engraved image or carving in the rock

21

SECRETS OF THE STONES

THE MYSTERY

Stonehenge is an ancient **monument** on Salisbury Plain. There are many ideas suggesting what it was for.

- Was it a place of **worship**— like a church?
- Was it a place to study the Sun and **astronomy**?

Was Stonehenge a **UFO** landing site?

One of the most mysterious places on Earth is Stonehenge, in the southwest of Britain. Once again, the county of Wiltshire is the home to strange energy. The mystery is not just about why, how, and when the great slabs of stone were put together. It is also about the feelings that some people have in this area. Many report feelings of strange powers around them.

STONE CIRCLES

Stone circles were built thousands of years ago. Many of the remains can be found in Britain, Ireland, and France. But Stonehenge is different. This ring of huge slabs has not been very damaged by time. It is still a place of power and mystery.

WEIRD WORDS **Druid** ancient religion of Celtic Great Britain
monument building or structure built for a reason

WONDER

About 4,000 years ago, the stones were brought to the site. Slabs weighing more than 25 tons came from 20 miles (32 kilometers) away. It would have been a major **project** to get them there. How did **ancient** people do it? Experts think they must have dragged them on wooden sleds. Before the first stone could be moved, a road had to be cleared through a thick forest. It would not have been an easy job. The ring of huge stones was a very special place. It has been a place of mystery and wonder for many centuries, and it will always be.

KEY QUESTIONS

Was this a place of human **sacrifice?** Some people think the **Druids** used Stonehenge as a place to tie a **victim** onto a slab and bring down the knife. . . . It is all very interesting, but in fact there is little to link the early Druids to Stonehenge.

Each stone is about 20 feet (6 meters) tall. **>>**

project   long-term plan or scheme
sacrifice   killing of an animal or person as an offering

A SUDDEN END

Over 1,000 statues were made from volcanic rock on Easter Island. Then they were somehow moved up to 14 miles (22 kilometers) away. The great **project** was almost finished, and the thousands of islanders seemed to be gaining in skill. Then something went terribly wrong . . . .

EASTER ISLAND MYSTERY

Easter Island has been called the most **remote** spot on Earth. It is in the South Pacific, thousands of miles from any **mainland.** The Dutch discovered it in 1722, on Easter Sunday. But its real mystery is the original island people and what they left behind. Around 1,500 years ago, the island was a **thriving** place. Its people carved hundreds of giant statues from the rock. Somehow the people moved these stone carvings across the island to where they now stand above the beaches. But the statues did not guard the people very well. Most of the islanders were going to die.

mainland   large area of land or continent
remote   far away from people

TRAGIC

The giant statues were never finished. **Tribes** on the island began to fight each other. Then, in 1862, a slave ship took most of the islanders away to Peru. A few returned and brought back the disease smallpox. The original islanders were nearly wiped out. There was no one left who could read the strange writing carved on the slabs. They remain unread today. Perhaps the writing answers many of the mysteries of the island. Where did its first people come from? Why did they carve the statues? How did they shape and move them? Only the statues themselves know, as they still look out across this tragic island.

MOAI

It is unclear why the islanders made the statues on such a massive scale. The carved stone heads are called moai. For some reason, none of them looks out at the water. They make an almost unbroken line along the coast of Easter Island.

Some of the moai weigh over 33 tons and are 23 feet (7 meters) tall. ❝❝

thrive   to grow in strength and do very well

THE MEANING OF THE ROUND STONES

The mystery stone balls left many questions behind:

- Were they part of a big model of the stars and planets?
- Were they left from a lost city?
- Were they rolled there as some kind of **ceremony** or sport?

ROLLING STONES

In the 1930s, the jungle was being cleared in Costa Rica in Central America. People found thousands of stone balls buried in the jungle undergrowth. The stone balls were made of granite, which was not naturally found in this area. Were the stones rolled there? The stones were all different of sizes.

Each stone was carved into a perfect ball. So where did they come from? Who made them and why? They are yet another mystery from the past. They are likely to be thousands of years old, but no one knows why they were just scattered deep in the thick jungle.

Some of the stones were as big as 10 feet (3 meters) across and weighed 3 tons.

ceremony   special event

DEATH VALLEY STONES

In California there are dried-up lakebeds that are now just flat stretches of clay. But strange things happen on the lakebeds when no one is looking. Huge stones move across them. They leave tracks across the dry mud. But the big question is: Why? Is someone trying to tell us something?

Boulders that weigh over 660 pounds (300 kilograms) do not usually slide on their own. There are no slippery slopes on these desert plains. Some scientists think the wind can blow the rocks. Perhaps rain makes the mud very slippery. Or maybe the rocks slip on ice. But this part of the world rarely sees water or ice. So what is going on?

THE RACETRACK PLAYA

Death Valley in California has less than 2 in. (5 cm) of rain a year. The ground can reach 135 °F (57 °C). That is very hot and dry. The dried-up lakes are called playas. The Racetrack Playa is where the mysterious sliding boulders are found.

Are these boulders really moving on their own? ◄◄

POWER OF THE PYRAMIDS

SECRET OF THE SPHINX

A huge stone statue of a sphinx guards the pyramids. A sphinx has a human head and a lion's body. The age of the Sphinx is a mystery. Wind and rain have eaten it away. Some experts think it could be more than 4,500 years old.

The **pyramids** of Egypt continue to have a special magic 4,500 years after they were built. These huge **monuments** have amazed people across the ages. They are full of wonder and mystery. Despite their age, there are still plenty of questions about the pyramids that remain unanswered. There also seem to be darker secrets to uncover, and there are stories of **curses.** These huge signs in the desert will always make our imaginations run wild.

> ## Fast Fact
> The pyramids were built as **burial tombs** for **ancient** Egyptian kings and queens. They believed they took everything with them to an **afterlife** when they died. That is why their riches were buried with them.

This huge statue guards the pyramids in Egypt. **‹‹**

WEIRD WORDS   afterlife   life after death
burial tomb   sealed room in which dead bodies are buried

WHERE DID THE SKILL COME FROM?

Robbers have ripped out the treasures from the pyramids over the years. The tunnels, chambers, and **vents** are now bare. But the design of the pyramids remains a work of **genius**. Yet that is not all. They were built in such a way that they line up with certain stars and planets. Who worked out all the math? Did ancient Egyptians have better skills than us? Did they have help from somewhere? We will never be sure of the answers. Everyone who looks up at the three pyramids at Giza and their millions of blocks of stone must ask the same question. How did they do it?

INSIDE

The Egyptians thought of everything. They knew thieves would be a problem. That is why there are mazes of dark passages, dead ends, and hidden rooms inside the pyramids. Burial chambers were sealed with huge granite blocks . . . and maybe the occasional curse.

genius   amazing mix of skill, ability, and power
vent   narrow chimney to help air circulation

MIND-BOGGLING

The Great Pyramid is as high as a 42-story building. It was made from two and a half million stone slabs, without the aid of **precise** tools for measuring or cutting. That is impressive work.

HIDDEN MEANINGS

There is far more to the three **pyramids** of Giza than meets the eye. Before raiders stripped the smooth outer stone from these pyramids, they would have looked even more stunning. The white limestone casing was stolen for buildings in Cairo, the capital of Egypt.

At first sight, the three pyramids seem to be built in no special order. The writer Robert Bauval discovered that their pattern was an exact match to the stars in **Orion's belt.** These stars were **sacred** to the Egyptians. The **vent** in the top of the Great Pyramid was lined up with the Orion **constellation**—maybe to let the dead king's soul fly up to its resting place in the heavens.

It would have taken over 20,000 workers to build the pyramids. But there is no trace of their living area!

constellation   group of stars
Orion's belt   three bright stars in a short line

THE GREAT PYRAMID

Some people find it hard to believe that the Egyptians built the pyramids just with armies of slaves. It would have taken many years. In fact, some say we could not build the pyramids today, even with modern machines. Will any of today's buildings last for thousands of years?

Whoever built the Great Pyramid knew Earth well. They knew math, science, engineering, and **astronomy.** The Great Pyramid's position was **vital.** For some reason, the builders wanted to leave something behind to last forever. Maybe the pyramids were just a sign to show how smart the builders were. If so, it worked—the world is still in wonder.

PRIME SITE

When all Earth's land is shown on a map, such as the one below, the Great Pyramid is at the very center. The math needed to put it right there, with its position to the stars, was outstanding. Was it just **coincidence**, or was there a superhuman brain behind it?

> The Great Pyramid lies at the center of a world map. Can it just be chance?

North America

Europe

Asia

Africa

South America

Key
▲ Great Pyramid

N
W ⊙ E
S

| 0 | 2,000 miles |

| 0 | 3,000 kilometers |

Australia

precise   detailed and very accurate
vital   really important

TUTANKHAMEN

The Egyptian pharaoh had been dead 3,200 years when his body was found. His gold was all around him. But his coffin may have been the biggest solid gold object ever made. It weighed over 2,400 pounds (1,100 kilograms).

Tutankhamen's burial mask with a **cobra** on its head was gold.

MYTHS AND MAGIC

Many strange stories spread about the **pyramids** of Egypt. Not only are the **monuments** themselves very special, but also what was inside: treasure and **mummies.** What more do you need for a good story? The pyramids make a great backdrop for adventure and horror movies.

CURSES

Myths began to spread once the tombs inside the pyramids were opened up. Strange writing on the walls inside was said to protect the bodies with a **curse:** "Those who enter this tomb will be visited by wings of death." This was a warning that bad things would happen to anyone who broke in.

canary   bright yellow songbird
cobra   poisonous snake

THE LEGEND

In 1923 Lord Carnarvon and his team found the tomb of the **pharaoh** Tutankhamen. It was the discovery of the century. A few weeks later, Carnarvon was dead. He died in his hotel in Egypt from a mosquito bite. It was said the lights went out in the town when he died. Back in Britain, his dog gave a howl and died. Five months later, Lord Carnarvon's brother died. The **rumors** grew of the mummy's curse.

When other members of Carnarvon's team died, the newspapers went wild. The curse of Tutankhamen made a great story. In fact, far more was made of the mystery than was really true.

A curse was said to be written inside Tutankhamen's tomb, and it soon became feared.

WINGS OF DEATH

Howard Carter was there at the opening of Tutankhamen's tomb. He lived for another seventeen years. But his pet **canary** did not. A cobra swallowed the bird on the day the tomb was opened. Is it a **coincidence** that what guards the head of Tutankhamen's mask is a gold cobra?

The cobra is part of Egyptian legend.

mummy   preserved body
pharaoh   Egyptian king

35

OTHER PYRAMIDS

One of the oldest and largest pyramids in the world is in Tibet: the White Pyramid. It is hidden away in the mountains, even though it is about 980 feet (300 meters) tall. China has over 100 pyramids. Many are thought to be older than those in Egypt.

BEYOND EGYPT

Pyramids do not just belong to Egypt. They were built in other parts of the world thousands of years ago. That in itself is a mystery. What made different peoples at different times and in different places build similar **monuments**?

GREAT MINDS THINK ALIKE

Deep in the jungle of Mexico are the mysterious temples and pyramids of the Maya. These amazing people mapped the stars, **invented** a writing system, and were masters of math. They built pyramids as high as a 20-story building—without metal tools—about 2,000 years ago. Just like Egypt's pyramids, those of Mexico are lined up with the stars and **solar system.** How amazing is that?

The pyramid at Chichen Itza in Mexico has 365 steps. That's one for each day of the year. **>>**

latitude   distance of a place (in degrees) north or south of the equator

LOST CITY ON THE MOUNTAIN

The Andes Mountains of Peru hide places of mystery. This was the land of the Inca people. They, too, built special temples to study the stars. Monuments like these helped them to plot the Sun in the sky. This was how they made their calendars.

The Inca began to **thrive** 800 years ago, and they were doing well until the Spanish came to Peru in the 1530s. The Spanish hunted the Inca down and killed them. But they did not find the Inca's special hideout high in the mountains. This was the secret city of Machu Picchu. Its ruins today show a place of great skill and beauty.

CHANCE?

It so happens that the pyramids of Egypt, Mexico, and Tibet are in line across Earth. Is it just chance that they are all at similar lines of **latitude**? Or does it show that pyramids are not just tombs, but signs to points in the sky?

The city of Machu Picchu was not found until 1911.

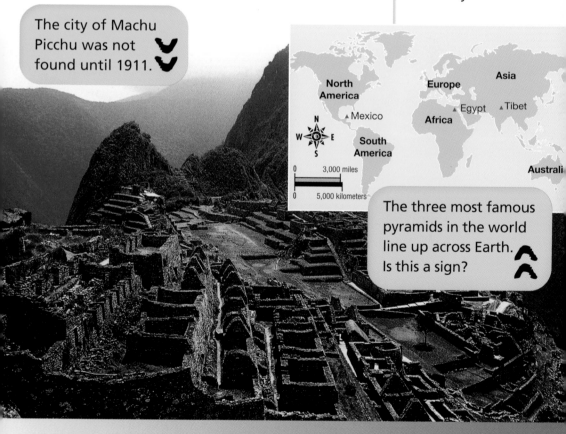

The three most famous pyramids in the world line up across Earth. Is this a sign?

MYSTERY OF THE MOUNDS

SIGNS ON THE HILL

People were not sure what all the bumps on the hill were at Sutton Hoo in Suffolk, England. In 1939 the bumps were dug open. They were buried ships. Anglo-Saxon kings and their treasure were buried inside. They had been there for 1,400 years.

Flat land is best for roads and houses. That is why we have always tried to level out all the humps and bumps. So why did people years ago make more bumps on Earth's surface? What were they up to?

GREAT SERPENT MOUND

The Great Serpent Mound in Adams County, Ohio, is a 1,311-foot- (400-meter-) long hill that is shaped like a snake. It is about 3.3 feet (1 meter) high. Native Americans probably made it around 1,500 years ago. They had to dig tons of earth from the valley below. A lot of work is required to make a sign that can only be seen clearly from the air.

No one really knows the purpose of the Great Serpent Mound in Ohio.

WEIRD WORDS   **burial mound**   ancient human-made hill with bodies buried inside

HUMPS

Silbury Hill is yet another mystery in Britain's crop-circle country, near Avebury. It is said to have a "powerful energy" around it, but no one knows why the hill is there.

Silbury Hill is the largest human-made mound in Europe. It must have taken 50 years to make. It is nearly 130 feet (40 meters) high and 550 feet (167 meters) across the base. The hill is a perfect circle. It could be even older than the **pyramids.** It is probably a **burial mound** linked to **worship** of some kind.

Perhaps Silbury Hill was used as a giant **sundial.**

CAHOKIA MOUNDS

Many Native American burial mounds are found in the U.S. The largest group, about 85 mounds, is in Cahokia, Illinois. Around 1100 C.E., about 20,000 Native Americans lived here. One strange mound even appears to have something like a stone pyramid inside.

sundial instrument for telling the time by the shadow of a pointer cast by the Sun

MAY THE FORCE BE WITH YOU

Earth's poles are like giant magnets. They drive unseen currents around the globe. Our upper **atmosphere** is charged with electric particles. Power is all around. Perhaps **dowsers,** who use twigs to find water, tune in to some of these mysterious pulses and signals.

LEY LINES

Some people say they can sense a kind of energy at **ancient** human-made hills or stone **monuments.** Perhaps such places were built on **invisible** lines of mysterious energy that run across Earth. These lines are often called **ley lines.**

ENERGY CHANNELS

In the 1920s, Alfred Watkins studied maps and old tracks. He noticed that **sacred** sites seemed to be joined by ley lines. Ancient peoples around the world appear to have believed in special lines linking their sacred places. It is as though channels of energy flow across the earth and meet at "power points" such as Stonehenge. In fact, modern science can sometimes measure energy bursts in these special places.

Dowsers use sticks to detect natural energy.

atmosphere layer of gases around Earth
dowser someone using sticks or rods to find water or minerals

LINES IN THE UNITED STATES

A lot of study has gone into these special lines in the United States. One of them is called the Hopewell Highway of Ohio. It is said to run from the Great Circle Mound, Newark, as a spirit path. This is like a ley line.

Some Native Americans have believed in such sacred trails for centuries. The Hopi of Arizona believe in an Earth Spirit. When crop circles appeared thousands of miles away, they said these were **symbols** of the Earth Spirit. So perhaps ancient sites, Earth's energy, and crop circles are all linked. Are they just signs of deeper mysteries we have yet to explore?

ULURU

Uluru, or Ayer's Rock, is a huge mound in central Australia. It has been sacred to the Aboriginal people for centuries. They, too, talk of "dreaming tracks" that join such sacred places. Sometimes they have followed them to find new places to live, led by Earth's spirit.

The Great Circle Mound in Newark, Ohio, has been made into a golf course.

ley lines invisible lines that are said to run across the landscape; thought by some to be lines of mysterious energy

DINOSAUR VALLEY, TEXAS

Huge beasts left tracks in mud, which then became fossils in solid rock. These are signs that help us understand mysteries of the past. Not long ago we knew nothing about the world of dinosaurs. The rocks are now unlocking their secrets.

SIGNS INSIDE THE STONES

Signs from the past have been left not just on hills, but also inside them. Rocks and stones can tell us about our planet thousands of years ago. They can also raise new mysteries.

LOCKED IN THE ROCK

Rocks in the Nevada Canyon are over 160 million years old. **Fossils** of creatures from that time are locked inside the rock. These creatures lived long before humans ever walked on Earth. Yet in 1927, a print of a human shoe was found in this **ancient** rock. How did it get there? Some say it cannot be a fossil, while others think it is proof that humanlike beings once walked this planet long ago.

Signs on the rocks of Dinosaur Valley help scientists learn about these creatures.

How did Egyptian carvings end up in Australia? >>

fossil   remains of an animal from long ago

SIGNS ON THE STONES

Australia has a real rock mystery. At Gosford in the Hunter Valley, there are old Egyptian signs carved on two rock walls facing each other in a narrow **gorge.** The rocks are covered in Egyptian-like pictures and **symbols.** People have known about them for 100 years and think the ancient Egyptians drew them thousands of years ago. But the big question is: What were Egyptians doing in Australia? And what were they trying to say? The pictures are nothing like the ancient art of Aboriginal Australians.

Some people think the carvings are fake. But the mystery still remains.

STONE LAUNCH PADS?

Baalbeck is an ancient city in Lebanon. The Romans built huge temples there with the biggest stone slabs ever made. One is about 1,100 tons and stands at the **quarry.** How were they ever moved?

Some people say the slabs were platforms for **alien** spaceships.

gorge   steep, narrow, and rocky valley
quarry   where stone is cut out of the ground or from a cliff

DENTS AND DIMPLES

ASTEROIDS

Sometimes an **asteroid** hits Earth. An asteroid is a huge mass of rock that orbits the Sun. It is like a small planet that can be up to 600 miles (965 kilometers) across. Luckily, only smaller asteroids have hit Earth so far.

Earth's surface is full of strange marks. There are huge holes and dents. For centuries people could only guess how they got there. Recent satellite pictures show their size. Now we can read the signs of how our planet has been attacked over the years.

BARRINGER CRATER

The Barringer **Crater** is a massive hole in the Arizona desert. It is nearly 1 mile (1.5 kilometers) wide and 650 feet (200 meters) deep. Its rim is made of smashed rock from inside the crater and rises 160 feet (50 meters) above the plain. Some lumps of rock are the size of houses. Its other name is "**Meteor** Crater," which tells us how it got there.

An asteroid just 985 feet (300 meters) in size could wipe out a whole country if it hit Earth.

asteroid   huge rock that orbits the Sun
crater   large hole in the ground caused by a meteorite

STAR WARS

Huge lumps of ice or rock fall from space. The **impact** on Earth can be enormous. It may be like hundreds of nuclear bombs going off at once. Some of the bigger craters from millions of years ago show the force that hit Earth. We have always been under attack from space.

About 120 craters have been identified on Earth. There may be more, but some craters have almost been worn away.

WOLFE CREEK, AUSTRALIA

Wolfe Creek sinks 164 feet (50 meters) below its rim. Like the Barringer Crater, this is just a dimple. It only happened a few thousand years ago. That is just like yesterday in Earth's millions of years of existence.

The Barringer Crater was formed a few thousand years ago when a meteor smashed into Earth.

SIGNS FROM SPACE

Satellites can show us the size of past mystery meteor craters.

Sudbury, Ontario, Canada

125 miles (200 kilometers) across
1,850 million years old

Chicxulub, Mexico

105 miles (170 kilometers) across
65 million years old

Acraman, Australia

100 miles (160 kilometers) across
570 million years old

impact   one body coming into contact with another
meteor   burning matter and dust from outer space

THE MYSTERY OF 1908

Less than a hundred years ago, a huge explosion rocked Russia. People in a **remote** village saw a fireball falling to Earth. Then came a bang, and the ground shook. The explosion was heard 500 miles (800 kilometers) away. Smoke poured into the sky. Although some people talked of a **UFO** crash, this could well have been an ice **meteorite.** That is because no remains were ever found. But no **crater** was left behind, either. That really was a mystery. But it did leave other mysterious signs behind.

ATTACK

Some people think that the dinosaurs were killed by a giant **asteroid** millions of years ago. The asteroid hit Earth and exploded. It released gases and dust that blocked out the Sun. Gases from the explosion mixed with rain and made it poisonous. All the dinosaurs died.

Whatever shook Tunguska in 1908 must have exploded in the air. Was it an **alien** spacecraft?

meteorite   large lump of rock, metal, or ice from space
nuclear   having to do with atomic reactions

SIGNS OF A BOMB

The **impact** area was called Tunguska. It took years for scientists to find the crash site. When they did, they were shocked. A huge forest had been burned and flattened. Thousands of trees had been thrown down like matchsticks in an area that stretched 55 miles (90 kilometers) in a fan shape. This was nothing like the **meteor** crater of Arizona. There was no doubt that great heat and energy had hit Earth. Also, levels of **radiation** were very high. It was just like the remains of a **nuclear** explosion. But nuclear bombs would not be made for another 35 years—at least, not on Earth.

This computer graphic shows the impact a meteor would have on Earth.

CHICXULUB, YUCATAN PENINSULA, MEXICO

NASA scientists think an asteroid about 10 miles (16 kilometers) across made a crater in Mexico 65 million years ago. The dust from the impact blotted out the Sun for about six months. The planet began to freeze.

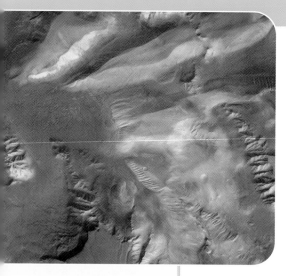

SIGNS ON MARS

Of all the planets, Mars has always been of special interest to us. That is because it is just next door. It is more like Earth than the other planets in the **solar system.** We used to think **aliens** lived there. We now know otherwise. Or do we? After all, we can see strange things on the surface of Mars that raise questions.

HILLS, CRATERS, OR SIGNS OF LIFE?

Some people think the photos of Mars, like the one above, show:

- great pyramids;
- a city with a fort;
- a ruin on a hill, like Machu Picchu;
- a crashed spacecraft;
- a row of huge slabs—like Stonehenge.

People used to think the lines that can be seen on Mars were canals or roads. Clearer pictures show that they are more like canyons. Perhaps they were made by water. And where there is water, there may be life.

NASA hopes to put humans on Mars by 2040. Perhaps they will unlock the mysteries of this planet's surface. >>

civilization   advanced and organized group of people

NEW DISCOVERIES

Space missions to Mars should soon find if there ever was life on Mars. An apple-size **meteorite** from Mars hit Earth long ago. Inside the meteorite, scientists found **fossils** of tiny cells. This could be the first sign that there was once life on Mars.

In 1976 **NASA's** Viking mission sent pictures back from Mars. One of them looks like a face. It looks looks similar to the Sphinx of Egypt. And nearby, there seem to be **pyramids.** Many people have studied the photo. They say it cannot be a trick of the light, since there is something solid there. It must be 2,130 feet (650 meters) high and 1 mile (1.5 kilometers) wide. But what is it?

WHAT DO THESE SIGNS MEAN?

- Does the "sphinx" of Mars prove there was once an alien **civilization** as great as our own?
- Did the builders of Earth's pyramids have "contacts" on other planets?

What do you think?

Look carefully at this photo of Mars's surface and you can see a mysterious face.

WHAT ON EARTH WILL WE LOOK LIKE?

FUTURE DANGER?

"

This is a **hazard** we can deal with and we must deal with. And remember, you are much less likely to die in an **asteroid impact** than you are in a car accident.

"

Duncan Steel, Vice President of the Spaceguard Center in Britain

Our planet is full of secrets, and it seems that it always will be so. Will we ever understand all the mysteries out there? Just as we solve some of those that puzzled our **ancestors,** we find more. It is only in the last 100 years that we have been able to fly. Since then, we have uncovered far more mysterious signs from our new bird's-eye view. In the last 50 years of space travel, we have found even more puzzles on our planet and beyond. What signs will our age leave behind? Some are already very worrying.

Just how will tomorrow's space travelers see Earth?

hazard   danger or risk

THE SCENE FROM ABOVE

Satellite photos already show us what we are doing to our planet.

- The rain forests are disappearing very fast.
- The holes in the **ozone layer** are growing because of pollution.
- The ice caps are melting and sea levels are rising.

But the future does not need to look so gloomy. We can already see the signs, and we know what we have to do. We just need to take care of our planet—a planet that has been handed down to us, with all its secrets from the past, and with all its mysterious energy. Perhaps the 21st century will begin to bring just a few of the answers.

COMING SOON...

An asteroid known as 4179 orbits Earth. It moves at 25 miles (40 kilometers) per second, and it is getting closer all the time. Some **astronomers** have figured out when it may strike. A news headline recently read:

World Ends on February 1, 2019 (possibly)

Our planet is more likely to be destroyed by pollution than an asteroid impact.

ozone layer   layer of gas around Earth that absorbs the Sun's radiation

51

FIND OUT MORE

WEBSITES

PYRAMIDS

Amazing site with information about the mysteries of ancient Egypt.
pbs.org/wgbh/nova/pyramid/

CROP CIRCLES

Photos and stories behind crop circles found in Canada.
CropCircleQuest.com

NAZCA LINES

The facts and mysteries behind these huge signs in Peru.
crystalinks.com/nasca.html

STONEHENGE

Read the history of the stones on the official site.
english-heritage.org.uk/stonehenge/

BOOKS

Mason, Paul. *Can Science Solve? The Mystery of Stone Circles*. Chicago: Heinemann, 2002.

Melett, Peter. *Pyramids*. Milwaukee: Gareth Stevens, 2003.

Oxlade, Chris, and Anita Ganeri. *Can Science Solve? The Mystery of Crop Circles*. Chicago: Heinemann, 2001.

WORLD WIDE WEB

If you want to find out more about mysterious signs, you can search the Internet using keywords such as these:

- "crop circle"
- mystery + sign
- ancient civilizations

You can also find your own keywords by using words from this book. Use the search tips on the next page to help you find the useful websites.

SEARCH TIPS

There are billions of pages on the Internet, so it can be difficult to find exactly what you are looking for. If you just type in "sign" on a search engine such as Google, you will get a list of 88 million web pages. These search skills will help you find useful websites more quickly:

- Know exactly what you want to find.
- Use simple keywords, not whole sentences.
- Use two to six keywords in a search.
- Be precise—only use names of people, places, or things.
- If you want to find words that go together, put quote marks around them.
- Use the "+" sign to add certain words—for example, typing "signs + earth" into the search box will help you find web pages related to mysterious markings.

WHERE TO SEARCH

SEARCH ENGINE

A search engine looks through the entire web and lists all the sites that match the words in the search box. The best matches are at the top of the list, on the first page. Try **google.com**.

SEARCH DIRECTORY

A search directory is like a library of websites. You can search by keyword or subject and browse through the different sites like you would look through books on a shelf. A good example is **yahooligans.com**.

GLOSSARY

afterlife   life after death

alien   being from out of this world

ancestors   people from the past from whom someone has descended

ancient   from a long time ago

asteroid   huge rock that orbits the Sun

astronomy   study of space and the night sky. A person who studies is astronomy is an astronomer.

atmosphere   layer of gases around Earth

baffle   to confuse and mystify

burial mound   ancient man-made hill with bodies buried inside

burial tomb   sealed room in which dead bodies are buried

canary   bright yellow songbird

ceremony   special event

civilization   advanced and organized group of people

cobra   poisonous snake

coincidence   when two or more seemingly related things happen at the same time or place

complex   very complicated

constellation   group of stars

crater   large hole in the ground caused by a meteorite

curse   strange power that is meant to bring harm to some people

dowser   someone who uses sticks or rods to find water or minerals

Druid   ancient religion of Celtic Great Britain

examine   to study something

fertility   ability to give birth or grow crops

foothills   low hills around the base of a mountain

fossil   remains of an animal from long ago

fraction   small part of the total

genius   amazing mix of skill, ability, and power

gorge   steep, narrow, rocky valley

gutter   groove or trough for draining away liquid

hazard   danger or risk

hoax   joke, trick, or something that is not real

humankind   human species over thousands of years

image   drawing or shape made to represent an object

impact   one body coming into contact with another at high speed

intaglio   engraved image or carving in rock

invent   to think up and develop

invisible   cannot be seen

latitude   distance of a place (in degrees) north or south of the equator

launch site place where a balloon or flying machine takes off

ley line invisible line that is said to run across the landscape, thought by some to be lines of mysterious energy

magnetic related to the forces of the North and South Poles

mainland large area of land or continent

meteor burning matter and dust from outer space

meteorite large lump of rock, metal, or ice from outer space

monument building or structure built for a reason

mummy preserved body

myth made-up tale, told over the years and passed on

NASA National Aeronautics and Space Administration (the U.S. space organization)

nuclear having to do with atomic reactions

observatory place to observe the planets, stars, Sun, and Moon

Orion's belt three bright stars in a short line

ozone layer layer of gas around Earth that absorbs the Sun's radiation

pharaoh Egyptian king

precise detailed and very accurate

project long-term plan or scheme

pyramid large stone monument with sloping sides and a point

quarry where stone is cut out of the ground or from a cliff

radiation invisible waves of energy that can be harmful in high doses

reed plant with tall stalks that grow in water

remote far away from people

rumor story based on gossip

sacred special in a religious way

sacrifice killing of an animal or person as an offering

solar system our group of planets that orbit the Sun

sundial instrument for telling the time by the shadow of a pointer cast by the Sun

symbol sign with a meaning

thrive to grow with strength and do very well

tribe group of people with similar beliefs who live together

UFO unidentified flying object

vent narrow chimney to help air circulation

victim person who gets hurt or killed

vital really important

whitewash white paint made of chalk and water

worship religious service or ceremony

INDEX